DOGMA DAZE

OR

How to Fight Back and Be Happy in Spite of it All

OTHER TITLES FROM FALCON PRESS

- Christopher S. Hyatt, Ph.D.
  Undoing Yourself With Energized Meditation & Other Devices
  Radical Undoing: The Complete Course for Undoing Yourself (DVDs)
  Energized Hypnosis (book, CDs & DVDs)
  To Lie Is Human: Not Getting Caught Is Divine
  The Psychopath's Bible: For the Extreme Individual
  Secrets of Western Tantra: The Sexuality of the Middle Path
- Christopher S. Hyatt, Ph.D. with contributions by Wm. S. Burroughs, Timothy Leary, Robert A. Wilson, et al.
  Rebels & Devils: The Psychology of Liberation
- S. Jason Black and Christopher S. Hyatt, Ph.D.
  Pacts With the Devil: A Chronicle of Sex, Blasphemy & Liberation
  Urban Voodoo: A Beginner's Guide to Afro-Caribbean Magic
- Lon Milo DuQuette & Christopher S. Hyatt, Ph.D.
  Aleister Crowley's Illustrated Goetia
- Christopher S. Hyatt, Ph.D. & Antero Alli
  A Modern Shaman's Guide to a Pregnant Universe
- Antero Alli
  Angel Tech: A Modern Shaman's Guide to Reality Selection
- Israel Regardie
  The Complete Golden Dawn System of Magic
  The Golden Dawn Audio CDs
- Joseph C. Lisiewski, Ph.D.
  Ceremonial Magic and the Power of Evocation
  Kabbalistic Cycles and the Mastery of Life
  Howlings from the Pit
- Peter J. Carroll
  The Chaos Magick Audio CDs
  PsyberMagick
- Sorceress Cagliastro
  Blood Sorcery Bible Volume 1: Rituals in Necromancy
- Steven Heller
  Monsters & Magical Sticks: There's No Such Thing As Hypnosis
- Jay Bremyer
  The Dance of Created Lights: A Sufi Tale
- K.B. Wells, Jr.
  The Montauk Files: Unearthing the Phoenix Conspiracy
  The Moldavite Enigma
- Phil Hine
  Condensed Chaos
  Prime Chaos
  The Pseudonomicon

For up-to-the-minute information on prices and availability,
please visit our website at
http://originalfalcon.com

DOGMA DAZE

Starring Freddie the Dogma Fighter

By
Christopher S. Hyatt, Ph.D.
and
S.L. Slaughter

THE *Original* FALCON PRESS
TEMPE, ARIZONA, U.S.A.

Copyright © 1982 C.E. by Christopher S. Hyatt and Stan Slaughter

All rights reserved. No part of this book, in part or in whole, may be reproduced, transmitted, or utilized, in any form or by any means, electronic or mechanical, including photocopying, recording, or by any information storage and retrieval system, without permission in writing from the publisher, except for brief quotations in critical articles, books and reviews.

International Standard Book Number: 978-1-935150-96-1 (Print Edition)
ISBN: 978-1-61869- 960-2 (mobi Edition)
ISBN: 978-1-61869-961-9 (ePub Edition)

First Edition 1982
Second Edition 2004
First eBook Edition 2013

Designed and Miss-Conceived by C.S. Hyatt and S.L. Slaughter

The paper used in this publication meets the minimum requirements of the American National Standard for Permanence of Paper for Printed Library Materials Z39.48-1984

Address all inquiries to:
The Original Falcon Press
1753 East Broadway Road #101-277
Tempe, AZ 85282 U.S.A.
(or)
PO Box 3540
Silver Springs, NV 89429 U.S.A.

website: http://www.originalfalcon.com
email: info@originalfalcon.com

DOGMA JUNKIES

Dogma is a drug—and we are dogma addicts.

"But Doctor, what is Dogma?" "Well my dear, dogma is acting as though you possess absolute truth, even though you have no real facts to support your propaganda. Some words which are similar are—dictatorial, stubborn, egotistical, bigoted, fanatical, intolerant, opinionated, overbearing, arrogant, stupid, despotic, and the list continues. But of course my dear, these terms do not apply to you."

From the day we were born we have been fed dogma by dogma pushers. This addiction has prevented many of us from feeling happy and living up to our highest potential. This addiction is so common that it often goes unnoticed, yet most of us desire a way to defend ourselves against the guilt and unhappiness that DOGMA creates. Dogma Daze provides a funny and helpful solution. ——IDENTIFY DOGMA——AND THEN FIGHT BACK! FIGHT DOGMA!

Unlike heroin, dogma costs you nothing, is not controlled by the FDA, since they don't control leisure drugs, and it can be found everywhere. Dogma is the freest commodity in the world. You can make Dogma connections without any fear of arrest. In fact not making proper dogma connections can get you jailed, and this could ruin your whole day.

Like heroin addicts we go into withdrawals when someone tries to take away our dogma. When this happens we go into a SURVIVAL —— ATTACK (also known as anxiety or fear).

DOGMA DAZE

7

Dogma is the *LSD* of the Status Quo —— and like LSD —— dogma creates hallucinations which we commonly share. This is normally called the "real" world.

The process of dogmatization is so important that institutions have been erected for the protection and dissemination of the Drug. To name just a few we have:

THE FDA

This group is involved with protecting you from drugs and additives which might harm you. Also they are involved with making sure that you are also protected against substances which might help you or save your life.

THE FTC

Here we are insured that competition between dogma dealers is fair and that no one conspires to fix prices be they lower, higher or the same. Their services also guarantee that outmoded ideas and products are not pushed out by better ones.

THE HEW

They insure that we all get an equally mediocre education and that our life styles don't exceed the standards of the bureaucrats who watch over us. In addition they are deeply involved in determining the minimum and maximum health and birth control standards for the population.

DOGMA DAZE

THE IRS

All comments relating to this organization have been deleted from this text, by order of the publisher.

THE FBI

No comment.

THE CIA

International dogma protection — this agency protects us against the dogma of other nations. According to some T.V. programs, the CIA will use any device conceivable to protect us from the insidious peril which is encroaching — — — — — — —
(Note: The publisher removed the remainder of the sentence.)

DOGMA DAZE 11

WHEN YOU GO OUT FOR DINNER, ORDER DOGMA

**WHEN YOU GO OUT ANYTIME ORDER DOGMA —
BECAUSE YOU WILL GET IT ANYWAY.**

AT LEAST YOU WILL FEEL IN CONTROL

If someone spots you going into dogma withdrawal (that is doing something which is a lot of fun) you will be provided with a remedy — be it sympathy — advice — or electro-shock therapy.

Dogma — Sometimes words are funny. Dogmatic people are often accused of playing God, and if you spell dogma backwards it spells -- AmGod. We often wonder if there is any hidden meaning in this "coincidence".

DOGMA SPEED

Dogma travels faster than the speed of light. If the speed of dogma transmission becomes slower than the speed of change, then a nervous breakdown can occur. When this happens, frantic attempts are made to find a fresh connection, such as a psychiatrist, who is a specialist in dogma breakdown and withdrawal. OR YOU CAN — watch T.V. Have an affair. Go on a shopping spree. Throw a war. Get sick. Provoke an economic disaster. If that is not enough, you can start your own counter-culture or, if you're really brave, you can start your own religion.

CREATING DOGMA DEMAND AND TRADE INS

Survival attacks can be programmed into your system by the Status Quo **DEALERS. Dealers motivate, foster and create survival attacks so they can feed you relief (i.e., Rolaids, Maalox, a new car, mouthwash, toothpaste, handiwipes, deodorant, Ex-lax etc.) They gently return you to an equilibrated, gas free state of DOGMA HIGH. This gives them credits in your DOGMA BANK which they can later call in -- particularly if they need you to do something which would be against your better judgment (such as getting killed in a DOGMA BATTLE -- wars, riots, etc.)**

ONWARD MEN! STRIKE NOW BEFORE THE INFIDELS CAN REACH OUR WOMEN!

DOGMA DAZE

INTELLIGENT DOGMA

The most advanced DOGMA JUNKIES are, of course, the educated addicts. They "CHOOSE" their – DOGMA --carefully, not knowing, of course, that they're junkies. They evaluate themselves and others in terms of the logic-reason-justice-originality and obvious truth of their DOGMA. Their customary paraphernalia includes style, value, convention, common sense, good taste, and consensus).

PUSHERS AND DEALERS

Dogma pushers and dealers come in various sizes and shapes, but at least 25% of the culture is in the direct business of pushing DOGMA free of obvious charges. The remaining 75% are in the business of creating demand and selling the junk for a "decent" profit. Dogma pushers are constantly selling, controlling and monopolizing the marketplace. If you shop carefully many of them give rebates. What Dogma have you bought today?

DOGMA ILLNESS

When better dogma threatens to take the place of worn-out dogma, the Old Pushers experience S$$$ur$$$vival -- Attacks. Without much warning they -- attack it -- kill it, jail it, ostracize it, or in some cases cure it (another word for Brain-Washing). The latest gimmick is a recent development used most openly in the USSR, and is normally labeled as "treatment." Instead of murder or torture, they "treat" those who wish to escape from dogma addiction. It is important to remember that an ill person is someone who has created a Survival Attack in the wrong person or group. When this happens, "experts" are called to provide the necessary treatment to "help" the victim back to health (PROPER DOGMA CONSUMPTION). Treatment also helps the patient become part of the FABRIC of Society. (Also known as useful, predictable and bored.) We are pleased to announce that this form of treatment will shortly be available to all.

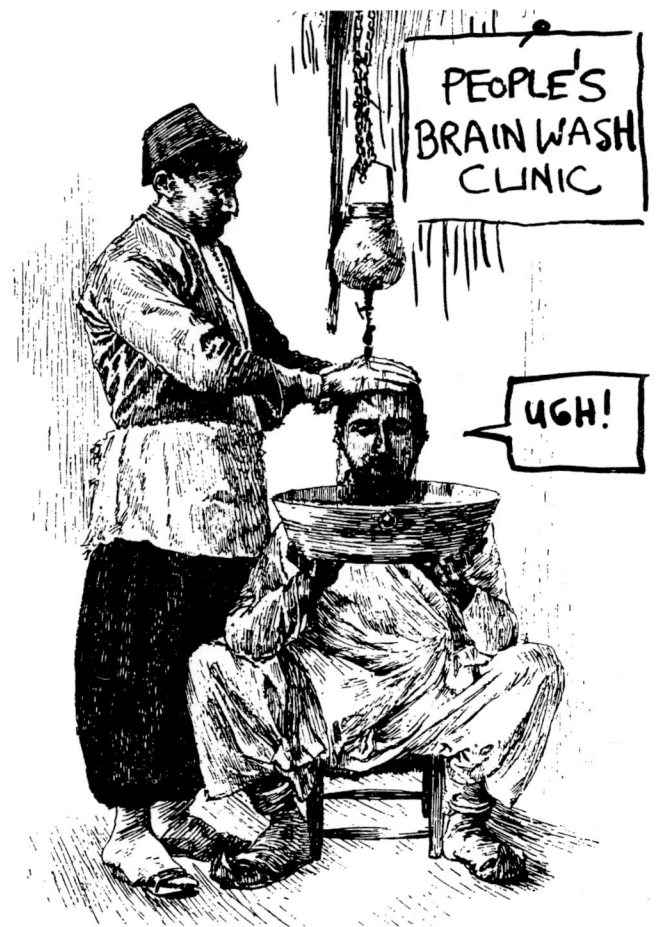

IN THE SEARCH FOR NEW CONNECTIONS

In the search for Dogma we find humans frantically running from place to place, person to person, belief to belief, doubt to doubt, pain to pain, euphoria to euphoria. They are doing everything in the world to prevent withdrawal and Survival Attacks.

For them to understand one another, and for you to protect yourself from their devices, a Dogma language is needed. We have reproduced a few choice words for your consumption:

DOGMA DAZE

1. CONSTIPATED DOGMA–MITES. These pesty creatures are always getting under your skin. You never know if they are insulting you or praising you. If you ask them a direct question they become insulted and look like they need a dose of EX-LAX.

2. DIARRHEA AM–GOD. Here you are constantly bombarded by words. They seem to never tire of proselytizing their particular brand of dogma. Often you feel like screaming, but instead you nod your head hoping that they will mistake you for a shrink and go away.

3. FOOD FOR DOGMA. Not you of course, only those who pay taxes, hold a steady job, and live a happy life in the land of the stifled.

DOGMA DAZE 21

4. RAW MATERIAL. This group includes infants, children and teen-agers, who are being processed to assume their role in the social palace of duty, boredom and conventional insanity (i.e., the mistaken majority).

5. DOGMA BUSTERS. This group of people consists of those who like to have fun and bravely try to help others to do the same. (In common language they are referred to as bad influences.)

DOGMA DAZE

6. DOGMA JUNKIES. Everyone, except you of course.

7. DOGMA PATROLLERS. Those in uniform and out. We are blessed with a never ending array of watchers and protectors. Are you one of them? Do you like to watch? If so drop us a line and tell us who you are watching and why?

8. DOGMA HEALERS. Those professionals that try to get you to fit in again when you finally start thinking for yourself.

9. DOGMA SCRIBES. They argue over the rights and wrongs of everything. More often than not they create more problems than they solve. This contributes to their income, for they are commonly known as lawyers and politicians.

DOGMA DAZE

10. **AM–GOD.** The teachers of unhappiness. This includes, but is not limited to, those whose vocabulary consists of words or phrases (75% more of which are) "right, wrong, can't, thou shall not, should, etc."

11. **BORN AGAIN DOGMA.** Recycled Dogma. Better known as a "fresh start" -- so you can repeat the same mistakes, but this time you can blame someone else.

12. DOGMA HEALTH. Those who believe that everyone must wear a size 12. They also believe that to be "good," we all must suffer equally. Don't buy this dogma no matter who says it. The truth is that one happy person does more good for the world than a million "serious", uptight, upright ——————— CENSORED

DOGMA DAZE

13. MARRIAGE. The ability to turn love and passion into A–BORED–DOG. A license to stop treating human beings like human beings. A decree which states that you must respect someone else's dirty habits, etc., etc.

14. FREE – LOVE. Sex without the benefit of boredom and in-laws.

15. HIGH HOPE. The Latest Dogma.

16. LOW HOPE. Moth-eaten Dogma not yet nostalgic.

17. DOGMA DAYS. National holiday where the Robots are allowed more time off without supervision so they can consume highly taxed and controlled substances and kill themselves on the highways. This provides extra income for the establishment through taxes, and raises the insurance premium for those of us who stay home.

18. SLUMMING. Visiting someone out of pity whose dogma is worn out or on a lower strata than your own.

19. FAIR DOGMA. I will give you a free lunch at McDonald's once a week for the rest of your life if you vote for me so I can have a free dinner at Spago for the rest of *my* life.

20. DOGMATISM. An invisible force-field which draws together people with similar dogma.

21. TEMPORARILY INSANE. Hospitalized dogma doubters who are getting "well" again.

22. ASSHOLE. A person who doesn't buy your dogma.

23. TAXES. Payment for government sponsored dogma.

24. IDENTITY CRISIS. When your T-shirt message to the world is being laundered.

25. DOGMA DEGREE. An authorized document stating what dogma you have been fed and tested on.

DOGMA DAZE 31

26. NOUVEAU DOGMA ATTACK. When you find out that no-one is reading the message on the bottom of your tennis shoes.

27. DESIGNER DOGMA. An item which carries the name of someone you don't know.

28. DOGMA SEX. Where you consult a table of random numbers to determine what date you will hop into bed.

29. EDUCATED SEX. Sex by the latest reference manual.

30. DOGMA DOLLARS. Something you put in the bank for your future, knowing each day as you grow older it grows less valuable. Of course it is "safe", and that allows you to sleep better.

32. DOG HOUSE. A place you pay for so you can feel secure in showing off your dogma in privacy, and assuring yourself an audience which won't insult you.

33. DOG. A creature which lives with you and does not question your dogma. This is why he is known as man's best friend.

PLAY DOGMA MAZE

DOGMA MAZE

This game is designed for those who want to do away with old dogma.

The person who completes the maze first wins.

EQUIPMENT

The board which is provided.
A die which is not provided.
The board pieces to match the characters can be anything you find as long as it's different from the other players.

THE RULES

Throw a die to see who goes first. The one with the lowest number wins. (AH! you see we are already doing away with old dogma.)

You can have up to four players.

The purpose of the game is to destroy old dogma and replace it with new -- fresh dogma. Each player should now pick a character. The character you pick determines your particular type of old dogma for this game.

There are four types of new dogma which you can choose to replace your present dogma -- (1) Anarchy -- This world is one of total freedom, with no rules, laws or regulations. (2) Law and Order -- This world consists of highly regulated and structured dogma, where everyone knows his place and knows exactly how to "live." (3) Mother Wit -- In this new world -- mother always knows best and all final decisions are made by her. (4) The Free Lunch -- Here everyone gets everything for nothing -- the only catch is that everyone must live the same type of lifestyle.

Choose your particular brand of dogma but don't tell the other players what it is.

The players should roll the die in order and move along the maze toward your unspoken goal. Oh! I forgot. Write down your original goal on a piece of paper and place it on the table so everyone knows where it is, but can't see your intention. As your turn comes up move toward your secret new dogma in a way which is not obvious to the other players. On your turn if you roll an even number you may challenge one player only as to her or his goal. If you are right, that person must start over again, if you are wrong you must start over again, so be careful. If you don't challenge a player just move the number of spaces on the die. One other thing: you can't challenge another player when he or she is in one of the safe areas known as Red Tape (marked "RT" on the board).

If you are challenged and you lose, take your piece of paper off the table, and write down another goal on another piece of paper. Continue to do this until someone reaches his chosen goal. The losers must now live under the rules of our new dictator's dogma until each and every one of the players say -- "GIVE."

THE CAST OF CHARACTERS

Diarrhea Am–God
Dogma Scribes
Dogma Junkies
Born Again Dogma
Dogma Patrollers
Dogma Busters
Raw Material

If you don't like any of these characters choose another from the book or make up your own.

DOGMA DAZE

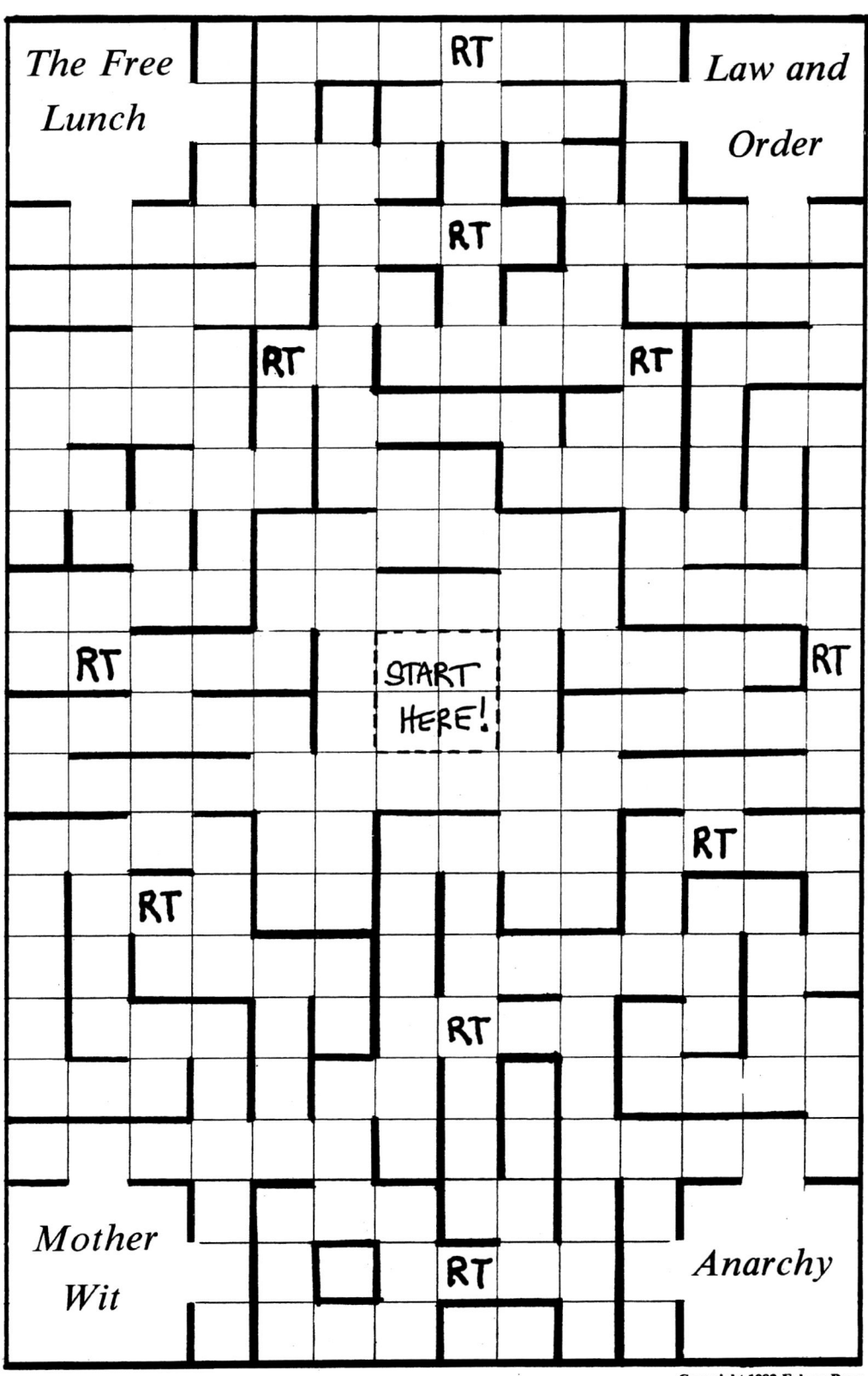

THE *Original* FALCON PRESS
Publisher of Controversial Books, Audios and Videos
Invites You to Visit Our Website:
http://originalfalcon.com

At our website you can:

- Browse the online catalog of all of our great titles
- Find out what's available and what's out of stock
- Get special discounts
- Order our titles through our secure online server
- Find products not available anywhere else including:
  – One of a kind and limited availability products
  – Special packages
  – Special pricing
- Get free gifts
- Join our email list for advance notice of New Releases and Special Offers
- Find out about book signings and author events
- Send email to our authors
- Read excerpts of many of our titles
- Find links to our authors' websites
- Discover links to other weird and wonderful sites
- And much, much more

Get online today at http://originalfalcon.com